Roxy   Buddy   Max   Spot   SpiKE

For Ezzy and Levon
–J.H.

Library of Congress Cataloging-in-Publication Data is available.
ISBN 978-0-06-218964-6 (trade bdg.)

The artist used Adobe Illustrator to create the digital illustrations for this book.
Design by Martha Rago. Hand-lettering by James Horvath.
14 15 16 17 LP 10 9 8 7 6 5 4
❖
First Edition

James Horvath

Dig, Dogs, Dig

A Construction Tail

HARPER

An Imprint of HarperCollinsPublishers

Wake up, dogs.
You're going to be late.
The sun is up.
There's no time to wait.

Grab your gloves,
hard hats, and boots,
shovels, goggles,
and dirt-digging suits.

YAWN

Eat some breakfast
on the go.
Quickly, now.
You're moving too slow.

Hop in your trucks.

There's work to be done.

Get to the job site.

Run, dogs, run!

Down the road
and over the hill,
driving big trucks
takes plenty of skill.

Around the corner
and through the pass,
stop at the station
to fill up with gas.

Okay, dogs.
We're at the site.
There's lots to do
before it's night.

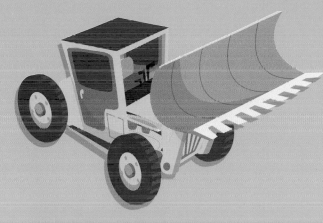

Start up the loader,

dump truck,

and grader,

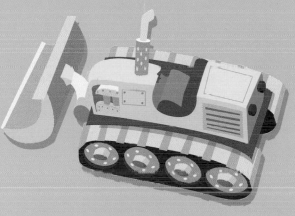

bulldozer,

backhoe,

and excavator.

The excavator digs deep
with its scoop,
pulling up dirt
with a swish and a swoop.

DOGS AT WORK

Push and plow
and clear the way—
the bulldozer makes it
look easy each day.

The loader picks up
a rocky big bite
and moves out the rubble
with all its might.

Hauling away dirt and sand,
gravel and rock,

the big, strong dump truck
works round the clock.

"There's trouble in the pit.
We've hit something big.
Get down in the hole and

dig, dogs, dig!"

Down in the pit
there's some busting to do,
with hammers, a pick,
and a rock splitter, too.

A job like this
calls for a crane,
with its winch and its hook
and its long, heavy chain.

It's a dinosaur fossil,
a huge T. rex bone!
With a tug it breaks loose
from its prehistoric home.

Now get back to work.

Get back to your crew.

Hurry up, dogs.

There's more work to do.

The graders perform

their dancelike maneuvers

as the ground is made smooth

by these heavy earth movers.

The cement mixer spins
as the concrete pours,
but there's no time to waste.
We're going to need more.

Sand, gravel, blocks,
and some 4x4 sticks.
The forklift comes over to
pick up the bricks.

Building has started.
Here come more big trucks,
hauling plants and trees
and even some ducks.

More equipment arrives.
Unload it with care.
Check it, unpack it,
and stack it right there.

Clear way for the flatbed.

Clear the way. Let him pass.

He's hauling our trees

and ten acres of grass.

More dogs arrive, with
ratchets and wrenches,
building fountains and fences,
bathrooms and benches.

Unpack the boxes.
Follow directions.

Make sure it's built right
so it passes inspection.

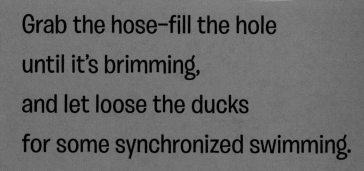

Grab the hose–fill the hole
until it's brimming,
and let loose the ducks
for some synchronized swimming.

Everything's finished.

What a day this has been.

Now open the gates

and let everyone in.

The workday is over.
It's now almost dark.
We have just enough time
to enjoy our new park.

Great work, crew. It's
a place all your own.
There's even a spot
for that dinosaur bone!

This job is complete.
We've built something new.
Tomorrow we'll find
a new job to do.

Duke   Roxy   Buddy   Max